SIR LANCE-A-LITTLE

and the
TERRIBLY
UGLY
TROLL

For Austin
R.I.

For Finley and Fred
K.M.

ORCHARD BOOKS
First published in Great Britain in 2016 by The Watts Publishing Group

3 5 7 9 10 8 6 4 2

Text © 2016 Rose Impey
Illustrations © Katharine McEwen 2016

The moral rights of the author and illustrator have been asserted.
All characters and events in this publication, other than those clearly in the public domain,
are fictitious and any resemblance to real persons, living or dead, is purely coincidental.

A CIP catalogue record for this book is available from the British Library.

ISBN 978 1 40832 523 0 (HB)
ISBN 978 1 40832 529 2 (PB)

Printed in China

MIX
Paper from
responsible sources
FSC® C104740

The paper and board used in this book are made from wood from responsible sources

Orchard Books
An imprint of Hachette Children's Group
Part of The Watts Publishing Group Limited
Carmelite House, 50 Victoria Embankment, London EC4Y 0DZ

An Hachette UK Company
www.hachette.co.uk
www.hachettechildrens.co.uk

and the
TERRIBLY
UGLY
TROLL

Rose Impey · Katharine McEwen

ORCHARD

Cast of Characters

Sir Lance-a-Little

Harold the Horse

Princess Plum

Huffalot the Dragon

The Terribly Ugly Troll

In the kingdom of Notalot there were not a lot of dragons, and by now Sir Lance-a-Little had fought most of them.

Diddums was barely more than a baby. And Sir Lance-a-Little was far too honourable to fight a baby, even a baby *dragon*.

Just go home!

And Bandylegs and Scabbytail
were both hundreds of years
old and had pretty well run out
of steam.

Only Huffalot was any kind of match for Sir Lance-a-Little. In fact, so far, he had never actually *defeated* the dragon. But *this* time he was determined he would!

For days Sir Lance-a-Little had been preparing: sharpening his sword …

and shining

his armour …

Now, finally, he was ready to face his No. 1 enemy.

Annoyingly, Sir Lance-a-Little couldn't find any parchment on which to write his challenge. So he sent his little cousin, Princess Plum, to deliver it *in person.*

"Go straight there," he said. "And tell Huffalot *to be prepared!*"

No short cuts this time!

Princess Plum set off, carrying a few cakes to nibble on the way.

But as soon as she was out of
sight, she looked for a short cut.
It took her over a rickety-rackety
bridge. A deep voice called out,
"Who's *that* skip-skipping over
my bridge?"

Princess Plum looked down and saw
a Terribly Ugly Troll.

"I'm Princess Plum," she said.
"I'm on my way to deliver an
important message from my cousin,
Sir Lance-a-Little,
who is following
close behind."

"This cousin, I suppose he's a lot *bigger* than you," growled the Terribly Ugly Troll.

"He's a *bit* bigger," she admitted.

"Then I'll wait for 'im," said the
troll. "You can go on your way."
So Princess Plum went on,
nibbling another cake, headed for
the dragon's cave.

By now, Sir Lance-a-Little had set off too. As he rode along he spotted a trail of cake crumbs leading off the path. He had a jolly good idea who had left it.

The little knight sighed and
followed it, wondering what trouble
his *troublesome* little cousin had got
into this time.

The trail soon led him across the same rickety-rackety bridge. A deep voice called out, "Who's *that* clip-clopping over *my* bridge?"

"It's me, Sir Lance-a-Little," he replied, "and I am on my way to fight a low-down dragon called Huffalot."

"I suppose this 'Uffalot is even
bigger than you?" growled the
Terribly Ugly Troll.

Sir Lance-a-Little agreed that he
was, but that wouldn't stop
him defeating the dragon,
he boasted.

The Terribly Ugly Troll didn't really care who won. He had an even better plan up his sleeve. He sent Sir Lance-a-Little on his way, planning to follow him.

But the clumsy troll was so noisy
that Sir Lance-a-Little soon knew
he was being followed. He had
no trouble losing the troll in
the woods.

Then the clever little knight hurried
on his way to keep his appointment
with the dragon.

The not-so-clever troll went round and round in circles, until he finally discovered Princess Plum's trail of cake crumbs. He followed it, all the way to Huffalot's cave.

When he arrived, Sir Lance-a-Little
and the dragon were already fighting.
"Who's winning?" asked the troll.
Princess Plum gave him a
hard little stare.

My cousin,
of course.

It was true, the little knight was running rings around the dragon. Princess Plum cheered him on. At first, so did the troll.

But soon Huffalot started fighting back, huffing and puffing for all he was worth.

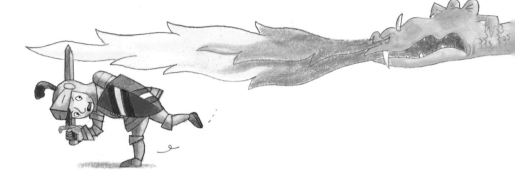

Now the Terribly Ugly Troll started cheering for the dragon. "Good 'uffing," he boomed.

"You should make up your mind whose side you're on," Princess Plum told him, crossly.

"Who cares?" growled the troll.

"I shall eat 'em both anyway."

When Sir Lance-a-Little and Huffalot heard this they stopped fighting *immediately*.

"Over my dead body," said Sir Lance-a-Little. Huffalot agreed. They turned to face the Terribly Ugly Troll.

"After you," said Sir Lance-a-Little, gallantly.

"Oh no, after *you*," said Huffalot.

Then the two sworn enemies chased the Terribly Ugly Troll all the way through the woods.

"Tomorrow, expect a new challenge,"
Sir Lance-a-Little warned the dragon.
"Not if I get in first," said the dragon,
determined to have the last word.

THE END

Join the bravest knight in Notalot for all his adventures!

Written by Rose Impey • Illustrated by Katharine McEwen

Orchard Books are available from all good bookshops, or can be ordered from our website:
www.orchardbooks.co.uk
or telephone 01235 400400, or fax 01235 400454.

Prices and availability are subject to change.